Eglin Long-
of
Nightshade County

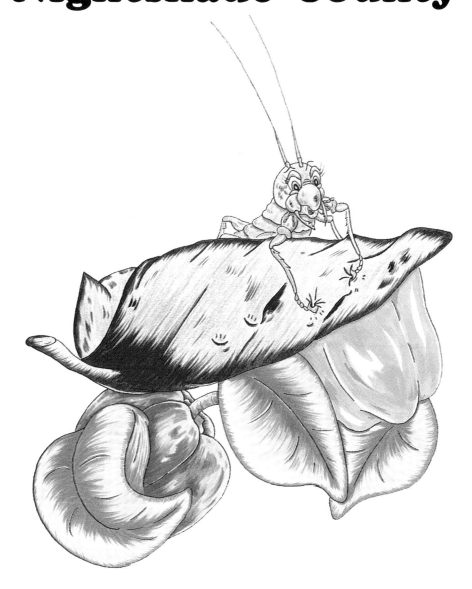

Written and Illustrated
by
Debra L. Wert

Rocky River Publishers
P.O. Box 1679
Shepherdstown, WV 25443
800-343-0686

The information in this book is based on the author's research of materials from sources such as the Florida Department of Education, Centers for Disease Control and Prevention (CDC), American Cancer Society, American Lung Association of Central Florida, American Heart Association, North Carolina Cooperative Extension, *The Marshall Cavendish Illustrated Encyclopedia of Plants and Earth Science*, and the 1992 EPA report titled "Respiratory Health Effects of Passive Smoking: Lung Cancer and Other Disorders." The author's appreciation is extended to the Winter Park Health Foundation for their support and assistance with this project.

Text and Illustrations Copyright ©1998 by Debra L. Wert.
Edited by Charles W. Wilson, Penny Wheeler, and Miriam Wilson.
Copy-edited by Eugene Lincoln.

First U.S. edition October 1998
Second Printing June 1999
Printed in Canada

Library of Congress Cataloging-in-Publication data

Wert, Debra L.
  Eglin Long-Horn of Nightshade County / written and illustrated
by Debra L. Wert. - - 1st U.S. ed.
    p. cm.
  SUMMARY: While visiting a family friend who lives in a tobacco
field, Eglin Long-Horn, the grasshopper, meets Varina, the ladybug, and
hears about the horrible consequences of using tobacco in any form.
    ISBN 0-94-457625-7 (softcover)
    I. Title
  PZ&.W477 Eg 1998
  [Fic] - - ddc21

                                                    98.45045
                                                        CIP
                                                        AC

ROCKY RIVER PUBLISHERS
P. O. Box 1679
Shepherdstown, WV 25443
(800) 343-0686

Preface

A Word With Parents and Teachers

Eglin Long-Horn of Nightshade County is designed to be read aloud by an adult to children nine to twelve years of age. Reading to children will give them the opportunity to ask questions and to receive answers at the appropriate times.

Due to the seriousness of this topic, the dangers of smoking, chewing, and dipping tobacco, I suggest that before reading this story to children you become familiar with the Teacher's Guide, especially pages 7 through 16, so you may effectively discuss this important topic with them. Through Eglin's story and helpful discussions, we can hopefully arm our children with enough knowledge to help them resist the temptations to smoke, chew, or dip tobacco.

Eglin Long-Horn of Nightshade County is a fable, a make-believe tale with characters that imitate the real-life dangers of smoking, chewing, and dipping tobacco products. Eglin's story is based, nearly in its entirety, on scientific facts. And so, while teaching a lesson concerning tobacco, *Eglin Long-Horn of Nightshade County* also includes lessons in entomology, critical thinking skills, reading, writing, and vocabulary. However, I must explain that, as an author, I have used some artistic license in choosing my characters. Although many animals can develop the same medical diseases as humans, it has never, to my knowledge, been studied and thus proved or disproved that insects develop these same diseases–specifically, cancer. Since Eglin's story is a fable—where insects speak, have feelings, family relationships, and friendships (which are not scientific realities for insects)—I felt it was safe to stretch the make-believe a little further in creating a make-believe tobacco field where grasshoppers, ladybugs, and beetles teach a very important and life-saving lesson.

Eglin Long-Horn of Nightshade County is meant to give young readers a better understanding of the dangers of smoking, chewing, and dipping tobacco. With this understanding will hopefully come the knowledge that smoking cigarettes, chewing tobacco, and dipping snuff can make people sick by damaging their lungs and hearts and making them vulnerable to cancer. And people do die from tobacco-related illnesses. It is my hope that once children have this knowledge, along with knowing the social negatives of using tobacco, they will make a pact with themselves never to start smoking, chewing, or dipping tobacco.

- The words in **bold** print in the story are listed in the Glossary on pages 64 - 66.

Dedication

To: Bootsy, Danny, Darra,
Brenda, and Michael

I love you. Please stop smoking.

Table of Contents

Chapter 1

Eglin Has Big Trouble

In a tobacco field in **Nightshade** County, a grasshopper by the name of Mrs. Ginny Long-Horn arrived for a visit with her cousin, Miss Florence Mole Cricket. It had been a long time since Ginny had traveled to the tobacco field. The tobacco field wasn't one of Ginny's favorite places. However, she had heard that Florence wasn't well, so she decided to make this special trip. Ginny was glad she had come.

Ginny brought her family of young long-horned grasshoppers to see Miss Florence. While Ginny and Florence gossiped about the latest field news, the **nymph** grasshoppers practiced their jumping. They were having a great time playing together. There was Eglin Long-Horn, the eldest, and best jumper; his brothers, Nicholas and Wilmington; and his sister, Olive.

It was late afternoon when Eglin decided to show his jumping skills to Miss Florence. At first he jumped among the leaves close to the ground. In no time at all he became more daring and leaped higher. He jumped so high that he landed on the very top of a tobacco plant. From his perch, Eglin looked around and saw rows and rows of tobacco plants. He saw the field sheds, too. And across the country road he spied the farmer's house and his vegetable garden. "You can see just about everything from up here," the young grasshopper called down to his family on the ground.

Suddenly the sky grew dark, and the wind blew violently. It whipped the tobacco plants back and forth on their stems as if they were dancing to the rhythm of wild music. Then rain came, pelting the leaves and Eglin too. It was a fierce storm. Before Eglin could jump to the safety of the ground, the wind snapped off the top of the tobacco plant and carried it and the grasshopper into the stormy sky.

"Aaaaaaaah," yelled Eglin. "Hhhhhelp!" he wailed. Then the leaf that Eglin clung to was ripped away from the other tobacco leaves. He and the leaf were tossed to the left and rolled to the right. The grasshopper held on for dear life. There was nothing he could do but ride the storm's angry wind. He was terribly frightened.

The storm carried Eglin past the field sheds. It twirled his tobacco leaf end over end and whirled him around until he was on the other side of the country road. The wind blew him past the big red barn where the horse lived. And it continued to push him straight for the farmhouse. The only thing between Eglin and the white house was the vegetable garden. What was Eglin going to do? He was on a collision course that would surely end with a splatter against the farmer's kitchen window.

The wind stopped as suddenly as it had started. Eglin's tobacco leaf stalled in midair. Then it glided slowly downward toward the vegetable garden. "Maybe I'm going to be just fine, after all," he whispered. Leaning to the left and then to the right, Eglin guided his leaf past the tomato plants and around the huge bell peppers. Down he came. Little by little the tobacco leaf lost speed until finally it gently bumped into a string-bean plant. Immediately the tobacco leaf fell with a PLOP and a small SPLAT as it landed on the muddy earth.

Before Eglin could sigh from relief, something round fell from above with another PLOP and another SPLAT as it too landed in the mud. "That's just wonderful, just wonderful!" complained the muddy glob. "I was very comfortable and dry and clean—before you bumped into my bean plant. Now look at me! Do you always make a clumsy entrance?" the female voice asked.

PLOP! SPLASH! A raindrop drenched the tiny glob. Slowly the mud washed away to reveal a splendid ladybug, who was quite upset with Eglin.

"At least I'm clean now! No thanks to you! Oh, just follow me. We need to find a dry place to wait until this storm passes," the ladybug said, giving orders to the young grasshopper. "Don't dally. Come with me, Pup."

The tiny ladybug's bossy manner made it clear that although she was small, she wasn't to be taken lightly. She was in command. In no time at all the ladybug had guided Eglin to a nearby squash plant. The two insects crawled out of the mud and to the top of a yellow squash fruit, where they found shelter beneath the hovering leaves.

"Who are you? Where did you come from?" the ladybug asked. "Why did you upset my string-bean plant?"

"I'm sorry I bumped into your plant," Eglin said. "I didn't mean to." Then he introduced himself and explained what had happened. He told the ladybug how the wind had carried him from the tobacco field and on his adventurous air ride. Worst of all, Eglin explained that he'd been separated from his family.

"Well, my little friend, that's quite a tale. Let me first say you have BIG TROUBLE. The tobacco field is no place for your family.

"There's danger there–and sickness. You've got to get your family away from tobacco," the ladybug said with great urgency. "The good news is–I'll help you. That's right, Varina is going to help you save your family. That's me, Varina. Are you with me so far, Pup?" she asked.

Eglin shook his head. He didn't understand at all. "What's happening in the tobacco field?" he asked. What's there that's dangerous and makes insects sick?" Worry lines covered his face. "Please tell me. My family's there. I must know!"

Chapter 2

Eglin's First Lessons About Tobacco

Varina took a deep breath before telling Eglin what she knew about tobacco. She didn't want to frighten him. She wanted to be honest and clear. "TOBACCO is in the field, of course!" Varina said confidently. "Tobacco can be chewed or smoked. There are over four thousand chemicals in tobacco and its smoke, and over four hundred of these chemicals are poisonous. One of the poisons in tobacco is called **nicotine**. Nicotine tricks the brain, just as cocaine and heroin, into thinking that it needs more tobacco to feel good. In other words, nicotine is an **addictive drug**."

"Over time, nicotine and the other poisons in tobacco can cause many kinds of illnesses," Varina continued. "For instance, tobacco causes lung diseases, including lung **cancer**. There are 43 substances in tobacco and tobacco smoke that cause cancers, such as mouth and throat cancers and cancer of the voice box. Tobacco is also a major cause of heart disease." She shook her head sadly. "TOBACCO IS VERY DANGEROUS!" Varina declared. "It can kill."

"Pardon me," interrupted a squash bug, leaning over the edge of a hovering leaf. "I couldn't help overhearing your conversation about tobacco.

14

Varina is right. Tobacco is dreadful. I heard the farmer crying while he and his wife were hoeing the garden the other day. He was crying because his son had just died from kidney cancer. His son had started smoking when he was a young teenager, even though it is against the law for minors to use tobacco. What a shame!" The squash bug sighed.

"How can tobacco cause kidney cancer?" Eglin asked as he turned his front legs, where his ear holes were located, toward the squash bug.

"From what I overheard," the bug continued, "the poisons in tobacco pass through the kidney and bladder before they leave the body. This means that people who use tobacco at any given time have tobacco poisons in their kidneys and bladders. The poisons build up and may eventually cause kidney and bladder cancers. That's what happened to the farmer's son," the squash bug said sadly. "He was very sick. The farmer and his wife are heartbroken."

Showing off a little, Varina spoke up, "Tobacco is the only natural place where scientists have found nicotine. Nicotine isn't a good thing. It's so deadly that farmers use nicotine to make **insecticides** to—" Varina gulped—"kill pests in gardens. If nicotine is in bug spray, it can't be safe for anyone to smoke or chew," Varina said.

"How do you know so much about tobacco?" Eglin asked.

Varina did not answer the grasshopper. Instead, she walked to the tip of the squash fruit and looked sadly up into the rain-filled sky. Her thoughts drifted away to another time and place.

"Now you did it!" the squash bug said. "She'll be gloomy for hours. Perhaps, I should answer your question. Listen carefully.

"Even though most insects and animals in Nightshade County don't use tobacco, Varina's family has been hit hard by tobacco and the sicknesses it can cause. Soon after she and a dozen brothers and sisters were hatched from their eggs, Varina learned her first lesson about tobacco," the squash bug explained. "You see, she and her siblings found themselves right in the middle of a tobacco leaf.

"I assume you know that nymph ladybugs don't look anything like adult ladybugs," the squash bug said. "They don't have black spots, they don't have red wing coverings, and, for that matter, they don't have wings. However, nymph ladybugs and adult ladybugs have one thing in common: They eat tiny insects called **aphids**.

"Aphids suck the juices from plant leaves and release a liquid from their bodies called honeydew. The honeydew is very sweet and makes aphids taste yummy. Nymph ladybugs have huge appetites and L-O-V-E aphids.

"Immediately after hatching, Varina and her brothers and sisters went straight to work, looking for food. And yes sirree, friend, they found food. The tobacco leaves were covered with aphids. However, these aphids weren't healthy. Instead of being a rosy pink or delicious green color, the aphids were brown. They were fat with tobacco juice, tobacco tar, nicotine, and all the other poisons found in tobacco. The aphids were tiny bombs loaded with tobacco's poisons."

The squash bug shook his head as he continued his story.

"The ladybug nymphs ate and ate the aphids. In no time at all, Varina's brothers and sisters were addicted to nicotine. All they wanted was the tobacco-fed aphids."

"Did Varina eat the aphids, too?" Eglin asked.

16

"No," the squash bug said. "Varina was too smart. When Varina saw the brown liquid oozing from the aphids' honeydew ducts, she knew something was wrong. She thought the brown honeydew looked and smelled disgusting. The aphids' breath smelled awful, too. Varina couldn't bring herself to eat the insects. The smell and brown color of the honeydew turned her appetite completely off. Varina didn't eat."

"How did she survive without eating aphids?" Eglin interrupted. "What happened to Varina's siblings? Are they still in the tobacco field?" the grasshopper asked, wanting the bug to finish Varina's story.

"A unicorn beetle flew Varina to the vegetable garden. Here she ate healthy aphids. When her wings developed, Varina went to see Dr. Walking-stick. She spent many days with him," the squash bug said. "The doctor told her about tobacco and the diseases it causes. When Varina had learned all that the doctor could teach her, she flew back to the tobacco field.

"What she found was heartbreaking," the bug said with a sigh. "Most of her siblings were sick with one of the illnesses caused by tobacco. You see, they'd continued to chase and eat the brown aphids. The tobacco poisons made them very sick. Also, her older brother had gone to the **curing shed** and never came home again.

"The curing shed is where the farmer dries the tobacco leaves before he takes them to market. There, Varina's brother learned from the mice who live in the shed, to smoke tobacco. Over time, smoking tobacco made his heart pump poorly, and it became clogged with his own blood. Varina heard that his heart just stopped.

"Some of Varina's other brothers and sisters have died too. One or two are still alive. However, nicotine has taken control of their lives. They won't leave the tobacco field for fear of never having tobacco-fed aphids again. They're not ready to give up tobacco. They may never be ready. Tobacco may make them sick first."

18

Eglin gasped in horror. "I will never use tobacco. What you have told me is dreadful. I understand Varina better, now. Thank you."

Suddenly he had a terrible thought: Miss Florence!

"Oh, no!" Eglin shouted. "Miss Florence has been chewing tobacco roots and putting nicotine and other poisons into her body for a long time. I must go back to the tobacco field and rescue my family."

"Varina," Eglin called, "let's go save my family. Are you coming?"

"Let's wait until the rain stops, Pup," Varina suggested, wiping raindrops from her wing coverings for a second time. "I don't want to get wet three times in the same afternoon."

So they waited. Later that evening Eglin stretched, feeling crowded in his skin. "It's time for a **molt**. My **exoskeleton** is awful tight. It's time for a new one." He hung upside down from one of the squash leaves and sucked in a huge gulp of air to force his skin to split open. Quickly he pulled himself out of his old skin. He slowly and gently pulled his long **antennae** free. This took a long time, as he didn't want to break them. Once they were free, Eglin pulled his antennae through his mouthparts to clean them before he settled down to eat his old exoskeleton.

"Look, Pup! You've grown. You've sprouted little wings," Varina shouted. "They're too small for flying right now. In a couple of molts, however, they'll be full-size. When this happens, you'll be a short-distance flyer. Before long you'll be all grown-up."

Chapter 3

The Journey Back

Returning to the tobacco field was more difficult than either Eglin or Varina had first thought. Varina could fly, but Eglin could not. Eglin could jump, but Varina could not. So with a naughty look in her eyes, Varina crawled on Eglin's back and ordered, "Jump, Pup. Jump! Jump as high and as far as you can. Jumping will be faster than walking! Jump! Jump! Jump, I say."

With a tight grip on Eglin's tiny wings, Varina rode the leaping grasshopper through the farmyard and toward the country road. "Jump, Pup! Jump!" Varina shouted again, just for the fun of it. She was having a good time. Up in the air they sailed; down to the ground they pounced. Over and over they went up in the air and down and then up and down once again. In no time at all they reached the country road. But crossing the road was dangerous. How could they reach the other side safely?

"I've got it!" Eglin boasted. "If you fly over the road, while I jump across," he explained, "you can watch for trucks and cars. If you see one coming, shout a warning, and I'll make my jumps longer and faster. It'll work. I know it will!" he said proudly.

And so the two friends crossed the country road together, one in the air, keeping watch, and the other leaping across as fast as he could. In just six big jumps Eglin made it across the country road. Varina made it, too. Working together, they had met their challenge head-on and conquered it. The long-horned grasshopper and ladybug were fast becoming friends.

As Eglin and Varina headed for the tobacco field, a mockingbird spotted Eglin. The bird decided that the grasshopper would be her next meal, so she swooped down and surprised the two insects. Varina immediately raised her red wing coverings and exposed the tiny wings underneath. She beat her wings and started to fly away. "Jump, Eglin! Jump! Find a place to hide before you're an afternoon snack. Hurry!"

Eglin was frantic. He hopped between blades of grass and among the field's weeds, trying to escape the bird's attacks. He leaped first in the direction of the country road, and then, cleverly turning around, he jumped back toward the tobacco field. No matter where Eglin jumped, however, the bird kept coming. In midair, the mockingbird changed direction and dove straight at Eglin. Then the mockingbird nipped one of Eglin's hind legs. "Ahhhhh," he shouted. Without even thinking about it, Eglin kicked the bird's beak with his free jumping leg. He hit the bird so hard that she staggered, loosening her grip. The grasshopper wriggled free. Eglin scurried away and scooted beneath the leaves of a weed. The bird recovered. She wasn't giving up easily. She ran along the ground, poking her beak here and there, searching for the long-horned grasshopper. Eglin crouched low, hoping she wouldn't find him.

"Hey, bird!" shouted Varina. "Why don't you chase me!" The mockingbird glanced her way, but for only a moment. She knew that the ladybird's red shell meant that she didn't taste good.

The bird returned to her search. However, Varina's trick had made it possible for Eglin to jump to the safety of a single tobacco plant that grew in the open field. There he hid among its leaves and tried to calm himself. Soon the mockingbird grew tired and flew away to find another insect for her afternoon meal.

Varina found Eglin a little frightened and a little sore from the mockingbird's attack. As she moved her legs across the sticky surface of the tobacco leaf, she said, "Let's rest in the shade of the leaves for a while."

"Excuse me!" said a white-fringed beetle in a garbled voice. "You're sitting on MY tobacco plant. If you please, remove yourselves at once," she ordered harshly.

Eglin quickly stepped backward to escape the beetle's bad breath. It was a foul smell. Eglin noticed that instead of having white hairs, this white-fringed beetle had stained, yellowish-brown hairs circling her mouth. He thought she looked nasty. The stains made the beetle appear dirty. Eglin also saw a large bulge coming from the inside of the beetle's jaw. It looked odd. Then the beetle did something disgusting. She spat a yucky brown liquid out of her mouth and over the edge of the tobacco leaf. Eglin could see that the leaves below were spotted with sticky brown puddles.

Feeling queasy from seeing the beetle's spit, Eglin explained. "My friend and I meant no harm. We are hiding from a bird who just tried to eat me. We need to rest. I promise, we won't stay long."

"Well, stay for a short time if you must. But don't eat my leaves," she demanded.

"You can count on that!" Varina said. "Tobacco is harmful. We don't want any of that killer weed! It will eventually make everyone who uses it sick. In fact, tobacco is probably the reason why you speak as if you have peas in your mouth. And tobacco makes your breath smell bad. **Tobacco tar** causes the nasty stains around your mouth and turns your claws yellow, too." Varina lifted her leg to show that the sticky tobacco tar was already clinging and staining the tiny claws at the tips of her legs.

The white-fringed beetle was clearly upset. Even though she knew Varina was right, the beetle tried to excuse herself. "I talk this way because I have sores in my mouth."

"And what do you suppose causes the sores? — TOBACCO!" Varina blasted at her before she could even reply. "Isn't that a **wad** of tobacco **chew** in your jaw?" she asked. "Well Beetle-bug, you should know the truth about chewing tobacco. It's mighty harmful. It sure is," she added.

Eglin pulled Varina aside. He cautioned her. "Don't attack the beetle because she chews tobacco. Instead, persuade her to stop. Tell her the truth about tobacco, but do it with kindness and compassion."

Varina whispered. "I didn't mean to yell at her for using tobacco! It's just so unwise to use tobacco. Everyone in today's world should know that tobacco causes sickness and death. But here she is still chewing. It's dim, just plain old dim."

"You know it's foolish, and now I know it's foolish, but apparently the beetle doesn't know it's foolish. Or at least she won't admit it. Be kinder when you speak with her," Eglin said.

Trying to be more understanding, Varina turned to the white-fringed beetle and said, "Let me tell you about tobacco. Chewing tobacco and **dipping snuff** can be more dangerous than smoking.

"Please listen to me Beetle-bug," Varina pleaded. "Nicotine is absorbed through the tissues in the mouth. When you put tobacco chew and snuff between the lining of your mouth and jaw, more nicotine enters your body than if you were smoking tobacco. Smoking is bad enough, but chewing and dipping mean even more nicotine, and that's not good. Chewing and dipping can lead to mouth, lip, tongue, and throat cancers. These are hard to cure because they spread quickly.

"I bet if I look inside your mouth right now," Varina continued, "I'd find the lining as wrinkled and leathery as an elephant's hide. Holding tobacco in your mouth irritates the mouth tissue and causes **elephant-hide disease**. It can take just a short time of chewing tobacco to develop this disease. Elephant-hide disease **(leukoplakia)** can become cancer of the mouth.

"Chewing tobacco also causes cancer of the cheek. This common cancer first appears as round, white ulcers. Over time the ulcers become worse and develop into cheek cancer. What does the inside of your mouth look like, Beetle-bug?" Varina asked the white-fringed beetle.

The beetle looked long and hard at Varina, trying to decide what to do. Then she did a good thing. She spat the tobacco wad over the edge of the tobacco leaf. She opened her mouth wide and asked, "Do you suppose these wrinkles and sores are elephant-hide disease or **cancer**? My mouthparts are awfully sore these days. Nothing I do seems to make them better. And I do want to get well."

"I'm not a doctor," Varina said. "However, these sores look pretty bad. The lining of your mouth does look like elephant-hide disease. I see that your **palps**, which you use to feel and taste food, have many white ulcers on their tips and along the inside edges. These sores could be the first signs of cancer."

In all of his days Eglin had never seen anything like the beetle's mouth. He took Varina aside and asked, "The white-fringed beetle is very sick, isn't she?"

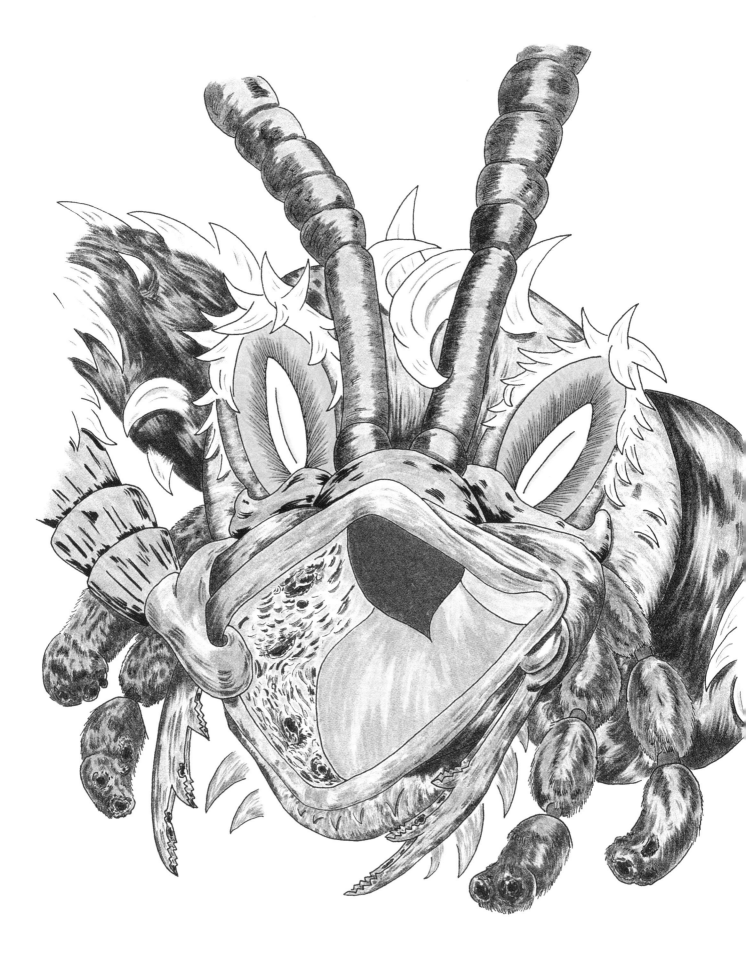

"Yes, she is very sick," Varina replied. "I hope she stops chewing tobacco today. If she doesn't, I'm afraid there's not much hope for her. I hate to see the beetle hurt herself this way."

Looking again at the beetle, the ladybug said, "You should see Dr. Walkingstick and let him look at your mouth. He'll know what to do. And Beetle-bug," Varina called as she and Eglin jumped away, "**STOP CHEWING TOBACCO!**"

Chapter 4

A Horrible Place to Visit

Darkness was beginning to settle upon the tobacco field as the two chums approached the curing shed. The ladybug suddenly became very nervous. Eglin knew the shed reminded Varina of her brother. Trying to calm his friend, Eglin draped his front leg around her spotted shell. "Everything will be okay. I won't let anything happen to you," he promised. As the insects stood in the doorway, a thick haze of smoke surrounded them. "What's that terrible smell?" Eglin asked as the smoke rushed into his **spiracles**, the tiny airholes he used to breathe.

"That, my friend, is tobacco smoke. Breathing it is very dangerous. It can harm our air passages and hearts. We must leave here at once," Varina ordered, turning to leave.

"Wait! I must learn the truth about tobacco," Eglin said, testing his will against Varina's.

Against her better judgment, Varina followed Eglin into the shed. The room was stuffy. A small smoldering fire glowed in a pit in the floor, filling the room with an eerie light. It was baffling as to why the fire was burning.

After all, it was too early in the season for the farmer to be drying tobacco. The tobacco was still in the fields. So why was the fire burning in the curing shed? It wasn't long before they learned the answer.

Off in the corner of the room Eglin noticed a flash of red light. Nudging Varina, he saw it again. Through the thick smoke the insects just could make out the faint movements of figures. As they crept closer they discovered a group of field mice. There were babies, youngsters, and adults. Some of the mice looked weak, a few spoke in raspy voices, and most were underweight. Odder still, the rodents coughed frequently, making loud hacking noises.

Eglin trembled, hoping the mice were too busy to think of a snack. Uneasy, he watched the oldest mouse sucking on a long stick. With each suck, a red glow flashed from the end. The other mice in the group worked busily, rolling dried tobacco leaves into sticks. They seemed stressed, for they nervously twitched their whiskers and tapped their tails. Then, one by one, the mice darted looks over their shoulders to see if the old mouse was watching them work. But she was too busy sucking her tobacco stick to be worried about her workers.

As soon as the sticks were rolled and stacked, Eglin saw a little mouse run toward the fire, dragging a tobacco stick. The mouse struggled, not with the stick, but because he couldn't breathe. When he finally reached the fire, the mouse doubled over, trying to inhale some air. Two male mice came to his rescue and carried their friend outside. Gasping for a very long time, the little mouse was at last able to clear his airways and breathe clean air into his lungs.

Soon the little mouse returned to the fire. He placed the tip of the tobacco stick into the flames, lighting the end. When the other mice returned to the group, one by one they sucked the burning tobacco into their lungs.

After a second or two they blew the smoke out. Again they sucked the poisons. Again they blew the smoke out.

The mice coughed and gasped for air. The little mouse gasped, too. He struggled to take air into his lungs. His two buddies rushed to take him outside again, and after an exhausting effort he was finally able to breathe. The other mice never even noticed he was gone. They just continued smoking the rolled tobacco. They did it over and over until the stick burned away. Then the mice lit another tobacco stick and smoked again.

Eglin noticed that the baby mice in the group looked small and sickly. Some of the young mice coughed frequently. Some rubbed their ears, complaining that their ears hurt. Others told their parents that their throats were sore. Still others wheezed just as the adults did, even though they were not smoking the tobacco sticks.

"What's the matter with these mice?" Eglin whispered. "Why would they suck smoke into their lungs? It doesn't make sense. Why would they put something so hurtful inside their bodies? Why?"

"The mice think they need to smoke," Varina said. "Nicotine is tricking their brains and making them think they *need* tobacco. Their bodies want more nicotine. At the same time, the other tobacco poisons are damaging their bodies and making them sick. The mice don't want to admit that tobacco smoke is destroying the air sacs in their lungs. They don't want to know that tobacco tar is turning their once healthy, pink lungs into sick, ugly black lungs. Of course, they ignore the fact that tobacco can cause **tumors** to grow on their lungs. And the tumors will eventually block their air passages so they can't breathe. No, they don't want to admit any of these things about tobacco.

"Tobacco is slowly killing them. The saddest part of all," the ladybug said, "is that most of them know tobacco is harmful. They simply aren't ready to ask for the help they need to give it up. Tobacco doesn't have to kill. We let it kill–by using it."

The oldest mouse decided to interrupt the two insects. But when she tried to speak, she coughed and struggled for a full minute before she could breathe enough oxygen into her lungs to utter a sound. Wheezing through each word, she offered a tobacco stick to the insects.

"Come, little buggies, have a smoke with us. I'm Madam Mouse. My friends and I are very nice company," she said, coughing into her front foot. When she moved her foot away, a spot of blood covered her foot pad. Everyone in the group saw it. Madam Mouse, however, ignored the blood and continued trying to persuade the insects to smoke. "Smoke with us, and we'll let you into our group. Come, sweeties, you'll fit right in. Come on, do it. You'll be one of us. Our tobacco sticks won't hurt you," she coaxed, smiling to show off her yellowish-brown teeth.

Eglin cringed at the sight of her nasty teeth. "No, thank you," he said firmly. "I don't want tobacco. I know it causes sickness. I'm healthy, and I plan to stay that way!"

"Oh, don't be a bore," Madam Mouse said. "Come on, it'll be fun. You'll look grown-up. You'll be just like us."

"No!" Varina said strongly. "We don't want to belong to your smoking group. We have many nonsmoking friends. They like us because we're kind and good insects, not because we smoke or don't smoke. We want to do more important, more fun things, with our time. Besides, we know tobacco kills! We're never going to start using tobacco. It's so simple: We're just never going to start smoking or chewing."

Remembering Eglin's caution, Varina softened her voice before stepping closer to the old mouse. Upon doing so, Varina could smell the mouse's fur. It reeked of smoke. Madam Mouse stunk! This time Varina's voice was kind. "Madam Mouse, smoking tobacco is damaging your health," she said sadly. "Look at yourself. Your teeth are yellowish-brown, you have bad breath, your fur smells like smoke, and your eyelids droop. I saw the blood on your foot pad, and it's most likely a sign of lung cancer. You're probably suffering from several tobacco illnesses," Varina told her. "Doesn't that worry you?"

Madam Mouse didn't answer, and the ladybug continued. "Madam Mouse, your heart may have been hurt too. Nicotine makes the heart beat faster than normal. This means your heart has to work harder. When your heart works harder, it sometimes becomes larger than it should be. This is not a good thing. And as often as you smoke, your heart muscle must be very tired. A worn-out heart is just a beat away from having a heart attack. Smoking will double your risk of heart disease. Nicotine also causes less blood to flow to your legs, feet, and tail. When these limbs don't get the blood and oxygen they need, they wither and die and sometimes must be cut off." Madam Mouse acted as if she was not listening and just looked at the floor.

"It can't be any clearer," Varina said, looking at the little mouse who couldn't run to the fire. "I've seen your illness before. The way you wheeze and gasp for air sounds like **emphysema** to me. That's a lung disease. Emphysema happens when the lungs can't expand and pull in enough air. The lungs can't release all the air, either. Stale air becomes trapped in the lungs, and breathing becomes more difficult.

"Smoking is a leading cause of emphysema," Varina continued. "Smoking coats the air sacs in the lungs with tobacco tar. Soon the air sacs become clogged and eventually are destroyed. Those who suffer from emphysema can't catch their breath, so they feel that they're suffocating. I think that's why you couldn't run to the fire, little fella. Go and see the mouse doctor. Go right now!"

Then Varina told the parent mice something that made them perk up and listen. "When you smoke around your children, you damage their health as well. Their natural defenses weaken, and they become sick more often. Children of smokers have more coughs, colds, and ear infections than children of nonsmokers. Your smoke and its poisons are drifting into their noses, throats, and lungs. This is called **secondhand smoke**. It is very dangerous. Poisons such as **formaldehyde**, **benzene**, **carbon monoxide**, and **nicotine** are in secondhand smoke. When you smoke around the little mice, you're putting their health at risk, too." Some of the adult mice looked surprised. Their whiskers twitched. They'd never heard this before.

"Please quit smoking," Varina pleaded. "It won't be easy. Take your youngsters and leave this shed. If you want to see them grow up, don't come back. Stop smoking tobacco today. Go to the mouse doctor and follow his instructions. In many cases your bodies can begin healing right away. It's never too late to stop using tobacco. Give yourselves and your children a chance for healthier lives."

Slowly Varina and Eglin watched as a few adult mice threw their tobacco sticks to the dirt floor. Then they nudged the young mice to leave the curing shed. One of the parents said as she left, "I'm going to stop smoking. I'm going to do this for myself and for my little mice."

A smaller group of mice still huddled near Madam Mouse. The old mouse was quite upset with Varina and turned her back on the insects. No one was going to tell her she couldn't smoke.

"Perhaps someday Madam Mouse, you will stop smoking," Varina said. "If you continue to smoke, however, I'm afraid you won't make it to the end of the season."

Madam Mouse's eyes narrowed with anger. "I'll get you and your friend for that," she said. "And when my mice get you, I'll let them eat your grasshopper pal. Get 'em, mice!" she ordered.

An explosion of mice raced toward Varina and Eglin. Varina, of course, could fly to a high, safe place. Eglin was not so lucky. As Varina flew past the harvest shears, Eglin followed, jumping on the dirt floor. He jumped past the shears, knocking them over, almost hitting a few of the mice. Then he squeezed between two buckets and hid in the tiny space. As the mice ran by, Eglin noticed that they were huffing and puffing. They were having a hard time breathing, and their pace slowed. He knew he could outrun them.

Quickly Eglin darted across the floor. After only a few jumps, he saw shadows moving across the wall, so he dashed behind a pile of charcoal. A moment later he looked to make sure it was safe, then he jumped out into the open once again. Quiet as the wind, he jumped to a stack of poles used in hanging tobacco. Eglin climbed to the top of the stack and looked around. He didn't see any mice. He did, however, find Varina waiting for him atop the tobacco sled. He jumped to the sled bed. "At last," he thought, "we're safe."

Then, from nowhere, four mice crept up and surprised them. At first it seemed the insects were cornered, but not so. Varina flew off again. As the mice dove for Eglin, he jumped over their heads and to the dirt floor, and jumped and jumped, trying to get away.

Turning a corner, suddenly Eglin found himself staring right into Madam Mouse's eyes. Her stare was evil, and Eglin shook with fright.

The old mouse snarled, showing her sharp yellowish-brown teeth. But just as she raised her curved claws to catch him, Varina flew by and tugged on Eglin's long antenna. Not knowing just why, Eglin jumped a mighty jump, and Varina steered him safely to a nearby barrel. Landing on top of the barrel next to a pair of tar-covered work gloves, both Eglin and Varina rested from exhaustion.

Knowing that the mice would soon find a way to reach them, Varina surveyed their surroundings. The first thing she saw was a photograph hanging on the wall. It was a magazine picture showing a lovely lady and gentleman. The lady was very pretty and elegant, too. But in her hand was a cigarette; an ugly, smelly cigarette.

"Look at this ad, Eglin," Varina said, tugging on his rear leg. "The tobacco advertisement is making it look as if a woman will be elegant, glamorous, and get her man if she smokes. The ad tries to make humans think that their lives will be filled with romance if they smoke cigarettes. The ad doesn't show that her skin will wrinkle earlier than normal, her teeth will turn yellow, and her breath, hair, and clothes will smell like smoke. It doesn't show that men who don't smoke may not want to kiss or hug her. This ad is a lie. Do you think humans believe these tricks? Or are they smart enough to figure out that tobacco can't make them look grown-up or bring love into their lives? We know tobacco can't do any of these things, but do the humans know it?"

Suddenly the two friends heard the scraping sounds of claws moving across wood. "The mice are climbing up the barrel," Varina shouted. "What are we going to do?"

Just as Eglin was about to throw one of the work gloves over the side of the barrel, hoping to make the mice fall, a barn owl swooped down from the rafters. "That's quite enough of this," the owl shouted at the mice. "Leave these insects alone! Go back to your corner right now or I'll eat you mice myself!"

Varina and Eglin stared in amazement
as the mice scurried down the barrel and returned
to their corner. The insects were safe. Or were they?

Chapter 5

Rose and Secondhand Smoke

Owls are natural enemies of long-horned grasshoppers, and at the sight of the barn owl, Eglin became frightened. He quickly found a shadow in which to hide. But he knew the owl wouldn't eat Varina. Ladybugs can release a smelly, bitter-tasting liquid from their bodies, and Varina's red shell would warn the owl that she didn't taste good. She'd be safe.

"Don't be afraid, little grasshopper. I won't eat you," the owl said. "Who-who-who said secondhand smoke is dangerous? Is it tru-u-ue?" she hooted.

"I said it," Varina spoke up. "Secondhand smoke is dangerous. It can make you sick! Secondhand smoke can cause lung cancer in nonsmokers. It also can cause eye irritation, headaches, and heart disease. In youngsters secondhand smoke can cause ear infections, and it can weaken their lungs so they develop **bronchitis**, **asthma**, and **pneumonia** more easily. It's dangerous, all right."

"My name is Rose," the owl said. "I've been in this curing shed for months. Perched high in the rafters day after day, I breathe the secondhand smoke from the burning tobacco sticks. The mice have been puffing on tobacco for a long time. They take leaves from each crop and hide them to smoke throughout the year."

"I haven't eaten any of the mice," Rose said. "They look too sickly. I thought that as long as I didn't smoke tobacco, it couldn't hurt me. I didn't realize that every time the mice smoke, I'm basically smoking, too. If that isn't bad enough, my feathers smell like smoke. A male owl who was interested in me as a mate said my feathers smelled bad. I lost him, and he found another owl for his mate."

A little upset, Rose flew off to circle the inside of the shed. She didn't want anyone to see her cry. Besides, she wanted to make sure the mice were behaving themselves and staying in their corner.

When the owl returned, she landed on the barrel with a clumsy thump and a short skid. She looked dreadful. Rose took deep breaths and held a wing over her chest while lifting the other wing to her head. She closed her eyes and didn't move. She waited before speaking. Something was wrong.

"Sometimes my heart pumps so fast that it feels as if it will jump out of my feathers. When I fly, even short distances, I feel a pain in my chest. The pain can be quite sharp. I can't always catch my breath," the owl whimpered. "Will I have to stop flying all together? Please tell me what to do."

Varina looked at Rose and said with a big sigh, "Dr. Walkingstick told me that one of the poisons in tobacco smoke is called carbon monoxide. This gas is the same vapor that comes out of the exhaust pipes of cars. It's deadly.

"When you breathe secondhand smoke, carbon monoxide is taken into your body. It enters your bloodstream and lowers the amount of oxygen going to your heart. At the same time, nicotine makes your heart pump faster. When this happens, your heart needs more oxygen, and it demands that your body give it more oxygen. But there isn't enough oxygen for your heart. Lack of oxygen causes the pain in your chest. The pain is your heart's way of telling you that it needs more oxygen," Varina told her sadly.

"Could I have heart disease from secondhand smoke?" the owl asked. She sounded frightened.

"You could," Varina answered. "You should visit the bird doctor. Ask her. She will know what to do. In the meantime, find a new home for yourself. This shed is an unhealthy place for you to live. Go now. Don't wait another minute."

Rose thanked the ladybug and flew out of the curing shed. She headed straight for the red barn where the horse lived. Varina smiled and whispered, "The red barn will make a nice home for Rose. I hope she sees the bird doctor and will be okay."

Standing just outside the curing shed in the silvery light of the moon, the ladybug wrinkled up her nose. She still smelled stale tobacco smoke. To her horror, it was she and Eglin who stunk! They smelled as bad as Madam Mouse. Not liking it one bit and knowing that smoking is not an acceptable behavior, Varina wanted to get rid of the smell before someone mistakenly thought that she used tobacco. So Varina flew and Eglin leaped to the honeysuckle vine growing nearby. After squeezing to get inside the closed flowers, they rolled and rubbed against the sweet perfumed petals. Before long Varina and Eglin smelled as sweet and clean as honeysuckle. Saying good night, the ladybug nuzzled among the flower petals, but Eglin, who liked the activities of the night, hopped off to find something tasty to eat. The nighttime atmosphere was filled with chirping and buzzing sounds as the ladybug rested and Eglin took his evening stroll.

Chapter 6

Chewing a Voice Away

The next afternoon Eglin and Varina entered the tobacco field not far from the curing shed. They jumped through rows and rows of tobacco. The plants were growing tall, and the leaves thick. Stopping for a moment, Varina noticed a faint aroma. Because her eyesight was poor, the ladybug relied on her antennae to pick up the scent. "It's an aphid! A green peach aphid, I believe," she said snapping her jaws.

Varina thought a green peach aphid would taste delicious. As she approached the small insect, however, she quickly changed her mind. "Oh, yuck!" she shouted. "That aphid has been sucking tobacco juice, and the tar and nicotine have poisoned it," she complained. "The tobacco has ruined my meal. I don't want to eat anything polluted by tobacco tar."

"That's fine with me," the aphid whispered softly. "I don't want you to eat me, anyway. I'd call my friends, the ants, to chase you away, but I can't shout any longer. Something has happened to my voice. I haven't been able to speak in more than a whisper for some time now."

Varina shook her head. She was sure this medical problem also was caused by tobacco. "Mr. Aphid, chewing tobacco and sucking tobacco juice from the leaves and then swallowing some of the juice can cause cancer of the voice box. You could lose your voice forever," the ladybug told him.

"You probably also have sores on your tongue and inside your mouth. Holding tobacco and its juices in your mouth can cause sores. May I see the inside of your mouth?" she asked politely.

Holding her breath so she wouldn't smell the aphid's bad breath, Varina inspected the tiny insect's mouth. Just as she had feared, she saw white spots surrounded by red angry tissue on the aphid's tongue. "I don't want to scare you," Varina said, trying to prepare the aphid for what she was about to say. "You have nasty sores on your tongue. They may be tongue cancer. You need to see Dr. Walkingstick. He may have to cut a part of your tongue away."

The aphid began to tremble. "I could lose my voice and my tongue because I chew tobacco and sometimes swallow the juice." he squeaked. "How can that be?"

"There are many poisons in tobacco that cause cancer," Eglin said. "In order to get rid of the cancer, sometimes the doctor must cut the infected area away. Go see the doctor before your voice and tongue become worse. Please go now," Eglin pleaded, just before he and Varina jumped away.

The long-horned grasshopper had gone only a short distance when he stopped in the middle of a furrow between two rows of tobacco plants. Here Eglin balanced himself and Varina on a blade of grass. The grasshopper was concerned for his family. He was beginning to see a pattern. Those who use tobacco can become very sick; some sicker than others. The more he learned about tobacco, the more frightened Eglin became. "Varina, what if Olive, Nicholas, or Wilmington become addicted to tobacco? What if they become sick? What if they—?"

Before Eglin could finish his sentence, a thunderous river of water came gushing towards them. It engulfed everything in its path. The furrow was quickly filling up with water. There was nowhere for Eglin to go. The water rushed closer, and he yelled, "Fly away Varina! Save yourself!"

"Jump out of here. Jump! Eglin, JUMP!" she shouted.

"I can't! Not this time! The grass is too flimsy. I can't push off! Fly to safety. The stem won't hold us both. Fly, Varina. Fly!"

As Varina took flight a wave of water slammed into the blade of grass and shook it violently. Eglin held on. With the skill of a gymnast, he walked up the piece of grass to escape. But the grass grew thinner toward its top, and with each step Eglin's weight caused it to bend. The grass arched and bent lower and lower until the tip just touched the water's surface. Eglin was very close to falling in. Wide-eyed, he watched the fast-moving water flow by. Then he had an idea. He took a few steps backward. Doing so, Eglin shifted his weight to the wider part of the grass stem. The arch relaxed and the stem rose, lifting the grasshopper away from the dangerous water.

"Whew! That was close," Eglin muttered to himself. Then, without warning, a second wave hit him and washed him into the cold stream. Eglin screamed as the water closed in around him. He struggled, paddling with all six of his legs, trying to raise himself to the surface. After what seemed an eternity Eglin's body popped out of the water high enough so his spiracles could breathe fresh air. An instant later he plunged back into the cold water, bobbing up and down. The current was strong, and it pulled him below the surface and down the furrow. His body jerked, trying to get air. His spiracles were filling up with liquid. His strong jumping legs pushed forcefully against the water, propelling him above the surface once more. Eglin coughed to squeeze the water from his airholes, and then he gasped, breathing in as much air as he could.

Eglin continued to bob up and down in the water, trying desperately to keep some of his airholes above the waterline. He looked for something to grab onto, but there was nothing. The water was moving fast. Eglin had no control as he swirled in its swift current. Soon his legs became too tired to move, and the water overcame him. He drifted down just below the water's surface. Just as he was beginning to faint away, something pulled on one of his long antennae. It pulled hard enough to give Eglin a small thread of hope. He kicked his jumping legs with every bit of strength he had left. In a jetting motion, he broke through the water's surface and inhaled as much air as his spiracles could hold. Then he saw through blurry eyes his friend, Varina. She was flying above the water and pulling him toward the furrow's edge. She had his antenna in her mouth and, with all her might and the help of the water's current, she guided her friend to safety.

Eglin lay on the wet ground for a long time. He was exhausted. Finally he whispered to Varina, "That was close. Thank you for saving my life. You're a good friend. Where do you suppose the water came from?" he asked.

"It must have come from the irrigation system. Usually the farmer turns it on, and water sprays like rain. A pipe must be broken somewhere close by. Will you be all right?" she asked her friend.

"I think so," he said. "But that was terrible. Now I have some idea of how a smoker feels when he can't breathe. I'll just sit here awhile and rest."

When Eglin recovered, he was hungry. He lazily walked along the furrow's edge to feed on some dandelions. The yellow flowers tasted delicious. After a while Eglin could feel his shell tighten. It was time for another molt. Not wanting to get caught in the furrow again, Eglin jumped high among the tobacco leaves and was soon tucked safely on the underside of a leaf, molting yet again.

Chapter 7

Families Meet Again

The next day Varina spent the morning hours sunning herself. When Eglin returned, he wasn't such a pup anymore. Overnight he had molted and grown into an adolescent grasshopper. Eglin's wings had grown, too. It wouldn't be long before he'd be able to fly.

Varina and Eglin moved deeper into the tobacco field. The twosome hadn't jumped far when Varina poked Eglin to stop. She saw something red. It was a ladybug. "Could it be one of my brothers or sisters?" she asked in a whisper.

The unknown ladybug had seven spots on its wing coverings, the same as Varina. It also was a deep red color, just like Varina. "It could be. It could be one of them," Varina hoped aloud. "It is!" she shouted as she hurried toward the bug, who looked just like her. Littleton, her youngest brother, recognized her immediately. He waved his antennae, signaling for someone else to come and greet Varina.

"Plata!" Varina shouted with joy as her sister poked her head from the underside of a tobacco leaf. "It's so good to see you. Are you well?" Varina asked. Unfortunately, she could see that Plata was not well at all.

Littleton explained that their other brothers and sisters were gone. Each of them had died from a tobacco-related disease. Listening closely, Varina became not only sad but concerned.

Littleton admitted that both he and Plata had health problems. Littleton suffered from stomach ulcers. The sores on the lining of his gut were caused by the juices he swallowed while eating aphids full of tobacco poisons. Littleton confessed that Dr. Walkingstick had told him that the ulcers could eventually heal and he could lower his chance of stomach cancer if he would stop eating the tobacco-poisoned aphids. The doctor also said that the ulcers could bleed and cause Littleton great pain. But so far, Littleton hadn't stopped eating the aphids.

Plata's sickness was more serious. She liked to hold snuff (ground tobacco) between her jaw and lip. The poisonous juices from the snuff caused sores on her jaw, palps, and inside her mouth. The sores had developed into cancer. Plata told Varina that Dr. Walkingstick had suggested an operation. He wanted to cut away some of Plata's mouthparts. This, he hoped, would get rid of the cancer. So far, Plata had not let Dr. Walkingstick perform the operation.

"Come with us," Varina suggested. "Leave this terrible tobacco behind. Come and live in the vegetable garden with Eglin and me. There are plenty of healthy aphids to eat, and Dr. Walkingstick lives close by in the old oak tree. He'll be able to treat you. I'll help take care of you. Please come with us. Once and for all, give up tobacco," Varina pleaded.

Littleton and Plata were scared about their health and futures, so they agreed to go with Varina and Eglin to the vegetable garden. Varina jumped for joy. She would do everything she could to help her siblings kick the tobacco habit and get well. Varina was going to have her brother and sister back. "What a happy day!" she sang to herself.

Littleton told Eglin that a family of long-horned grasshoppers were living nearby. Eglin immediately jumped and headed off in the direction of Littleton's point. Flying to catch up with him, Varina shouted to her brother and sister, "We'll be back for you as soon as we find Eglin's family. We'll be back!"

Excited by the thought of seeing his family again, Eglin jumped a little too fast and a little too recklessly from one tobacco leaf to another. Once he leaped so high that when he landed on the next leaf, Varina was gone. "Varina! Varina, where are you?" the confused grasshopper called. Then he heard grumbling.

"Here I am," Varina griped as she poked her head from the underside of a tobacco leaf. "I'm stuck. When you jumped so high, I was pushed into a bubble of tobacco tar oozing from this leaf. I'm stuck! Eglin, get me out!" Suddenly a breeze blew by, carrying a cluster of white fluffy dandelion seeds. Varina looked in horror as the seeds came straight for her. "NO!" she yelled. It was too late. The white, fluffy seeds glued themselves to Varina's head and wing coverings. She looked like a cross between a white-crested rooster and a fluffy porcupine.

Eglin roared with laughter. Varina looked so funny. The tar dripped from her head, and the white fluffy spikes seemed to grow out of her head and wing coverings. He laughed and laughed. What a sight!

"Help get this stuff off me!" Varina demanded. "Scientists have proven that tobacco tar dripped on the fur of mice can cause skin cancer. Please Eglin, get it off!"

Eglin took his friend to the ground and rubbed soft dirt on her red wing coverings and black head. He worked until the tar was gone.

However, Eglin left one fluffy spike sticking up on the top of her head. He just couldn't resist being a little naughty.

Eglin was the first to see his sister Olive. When he saw her face-to-face, his worst fear came true. Olive had a wad of tobacco chew stuffed between her jaw and lip. Yellowish-brown stains dripped down the outside of her mouth. The stains came from tobacco-juice drool. As Olive walked toward Eglin she spat a long stream of brown tobacco juice, almost hitting Varina. Eglin was worried. His baby sister was chewing tobacco.

The two long-horned grasshoppers hugged for a long time. As they parted, Eglin smelled Olive's bad breath. It was an old story by now. Those who chewed and smoked tobacco had a nasty smell. Even his adorable little sister had bad breath.

"I'm so disappointed, Olive," Eglin sighed. "Why did you start chewing tobacco? It's a disgusting habit. Don't you know that tobacco can make you terribly sick?" he asked. "Not to mention how ridiculous you look with a bulge in your mouth."

"Everyone here does it!" Olive protested. "I'm just doing what the other insects do. Some even go to the storage and curing sheds to learn how to smoke tobacco. At least I'm not smoking the stuff."

"First of all, little sister, chewing tobacco can be more harmful than smoking. I've just seen a white-fringed beetle and an aphid that have terrible mouth diseases because they chew tobacco. Secondly, not everyone is doing it! I've learned that most young and adult insects don't use tobacco. For that matter, most humans don't use it either! And just because others do reckless things such as smoking or chewing tobacco, do you have to do the same reckless things?" her big brother asked.

"No, of course, you don't!" Then Eglin softened his approach and tried again. He didn't want to yell at his sister. He wanted to persuade her to stop chewing.

"Olive, I want you to learn the truth about tobacco. Tobacco is harmful. Chewing it will cause sores to form on your tongue and lips and on the inside of your cheeks, jaw, and throat. The sores can develop into cancer. Tobacco can cause heart disease. Please give it up. Give up tobacco so you can live a healthier life. And if you won't stop for your health, then stop because it looks and smells bad.

"Do you think you're going to find a mate when you have bad breath, yellow stains in and around your mouth, and smell like tobacco? Olive, no tobacco-free long-horned grasshopper will find you attractive with tobacco breath and stains. Leave this field," Eglin pleaded. "Come with the family to the garden. It's nice there."

"What makes you think the family will leave the tobacco field? We might be happy here!" Olive declared.

"I'm hopeful that our family will leave this place," Eglin replied. "Oh, Olive, please give up tobacco. It can cause a whole bunch of pain. I don't want you to die before your life cycle is complete. Varina has lost all but two of her brothers and sisters because of tobacco illnesses. Please give up tobacco. Olive–PLEASE listen."

"You sound like Wilmington. He doesn't like it here, either," she confessed, spitting tobacco juice once again. "You two just don't want me to have any fun."

"FUN! Do you think putting poisons into your lungs and body is fun? It's not fun, it's not cool, it's not anything but–foolish!" Eglin cried. "At least Wilmington has the sense to know that tobacco is a harmful weed." Eglin said to his sister: "Where is the rest of the family, anyway? Where are Wilmington, Nicholas, and Mother?"

Chapter 8

Good-byes Are Too Often Tobacco's Fault

Olive led Eglin and Varina to the field's floor where Wilmington, Ginny, and Florence were resting beneath a tobacco plant. The reunion between Eglin and his mother and brother was joyous, but at the same time, sad. Something was seriously wrong with Florence Mole Cricket.

Eglin's mother explained their cousin's illness. "Yesterday Florence became very weak. The left side of her face and body went numb. When I asked her what was the matter, she couldn't tell me. Immediately, I jumped and flew to the old oak tree to see Dr. Walkingstick. He told me that it appeared as if Florence had a **stroke**, or **brain attack**. This happens when a blood vessel in the brain bursts or gets clogged. Part of the brain doesn't get the blood it needs and in minutes begins to die. That's why Florence can't speak properly or move her left side. Dr. Walkingstick said that most likely tobacco and its poisons are the cause of her stroke."

"I'll take Cousin Florence to Dr. Walkingstick so he can help her get well," Eglin offered.

"No!" Ginny said. "The end is near. She's ready to go, now."

Eglin shook his head and said, "In the past few days I've seen a white-fringed beetle, a green peach aphid, two ladybugs, and a whole group of mice suffer because of tobacco," he told his family. "Tobacco is the most harmful plant in the world. Look at what it's done to Florence." His eyes filled with tears. "Florence gave tobacco and nicotine the chance to make her sick—by chewing it."

"Olive, are you listening?" Eglin called to his sister. We don't want to lose you the way we're losing Cousin Florence."

"Mother," Eglin began, "our family must leave the tobacco field. Let's go to the vegetable garden with Varina and her siblings. The garden is a nice place. We can live healthy lives there."

Eglin's mother didn't answer. Suddenly he knew that she too had chewed the tobacco leaves. Ginny Long-Horn was getting used to the taste of tobacco. Or was she really becoming addicted to nicotine?

"Ah, Mother, not you too!" Eglin scolded. "How could you?"

Looking at his mother, Eglin became so frustrated with his family that he shouted, "Why can't any of you see that tobacco is addictive? It's full of poisons and will destroy your health and possibly kill you. Tobacco causes bad breath, and gums to pull away from teeth, causing tooth loss. It causes mouth sores. It grows cancer all over the body. Putting tobacco smoke and tar into your lungs causes emphysema, black lungs, and lung cancer. Tobacco causes heart disease. Can anyone tell me a good reason to use tobacco? I can't think of one good reason in the whole wide world to use tobacco!

"Please, Mother, stop chewing tobacco. It's never too late. I love you, Mother. I don't want you to end up like Cousin Florence. Please stop!" Eglin begged.

"D-d-doo as he s-s-says," Florence whispered, struggling to force the words from the right corner of her mouth. And then she closed her eyes and died.

Early the next morning the family of long-horned grasshoppers and their ladybug friend buried Cousin Florence Mole Cricket in the last tunnel she had dug before her stroke. Her body would decompose, giving nutrients back to the soil to help plants grow. Having covered her with soft dirt, Eglin announced, "It's time for us to leave the tobacco field. I can't wait to leave this place. I will never come back."

"I'm not leaving," Olive said boldly. "I've decided to stay."

"Olive, you can't be serious, Eglin responded. "How can you stay here after Florence's death? Don't you remember what I told you about the white-fringed beetle, the green peach aphid, and the mice. Don't stay. Tobacco will make you sick."

"Eglin, I'm staying," Olive said, spitting tobacco juice from her mouth. "Maybe someday I'll stop chewing on these tobacco leaves. When I do, I'll find you in the vegetable garden. But until I'm ready, I'm staying right here."

"Varina, speak with her," Eglin ordered. "Convince her to come with us."

"Eglin, I cannot," Varina confessed. "Olive has listened to the truth about using tobacco. After all the talk, we can only hope that she cares enough about her health to quit chewing. We are each responsible for our own health. No one but Olive can make this work. She must want to stop," Varina said.

"But it's wrong for her to chew," Eglin cried. "Oh Varina, it's so hard to watch someone you love hurt themselves. It's so hard."

The family of long-horned grasshoppers and what was left of Varina's family left the tobacco field, feeling both happy and sad. Eglin was more sad than happy. He had wanted to rescue his entire family. Instead, he was leaving behind both Olive and Nicholas. He was afraid that his family would never be together again.

Chapter 9

Choosing the Vegetable Garden

Life in the vegetable garden was calm and good. The air was fresh, there were plenty of healthy foods to eat, and there was no tobacco any-where around. Although Eglin's heart ached for Nicholas and Olive, he kept busy. Time passed quickly, and soon it was time for Eglin and Wilmington to molt for the last time. Eglin would soon become an adult grasshopper. And so he and Wilmington, under the cover of darkness, dangled from separate pepper leaves. Before long the two long-horned grasshoppers pulled their new, larger bodies from their old exoskeletons. Eglin and Wilmington were full-grown grasshoppers, ready to mate. As Eglin and his brother stretched, full-grown wings uncurled to dry. The grasshoppers had their wings. They were flyers.

The next afternoon Eglin found Varina feeding on some pink aphids. "Look, Varina!" Eglin shouted. "I'm all grown-up. You can't call me Pup anymore! I've got my wings! I can fly! We can fly together!"

In the midst of all the merriment, no one noticed the three long-horned grasshoppers who quietly walked below the bell pepper plants. When they heard Eglin's shouts, the three grasshoppers stopped and looked up into the thickset leaves. "Eglin, is that you?" a voice called.

Eglin stopped his shouting. He stared toward the ground in amazement. The small group of grasshoppers looked familiar. "It's Nicholas, my brother," he squealed. "Oh, Nicholas, I thought I'd never see you again!"

Joyously Eglin jumped high in the air, twirled a back flip, and landed on the soft ground next to his long-lost brother. "Where have you been?" he asked. "I've been worried about you."

Nicholas was happy to see Eglin, also. He lovingly touched his big brother's antennae and said, "I went searching for you, big brother. I couldn't leave you to the mercy of the storm. Besides, I couldn't stay in the tobacco field. I didn't want to start using tobacco. I knew that if I started, it would be mighty hard to stop. The best thing for me was never to start in the first place. So I built-up my courage and told Olive and her friends 'NO, I don't want tobacco.' Then I left the field to find you.

"Yesterday I found Olive alone and not well," Nicholas continued. "I've brought her here to be with the family. She wanted to come. She's ready to stop chewing tobacco."

Olive was leaning forward with her head lowered. She huffed and puffed, struggling to breathe after her long walk. Of course she was happy to see Eglin. She was a little embarrassed, too.

"Olive, I'm so very glad to see you," Eglin said to ease her way. "And Mother will be beside herself with joy. She's doing fine these days. Florence's death had a startling effect on Mother. Sometimes it takes a tragedy before one knows the right thing to do. Giving up tobacco was the best thing Mother ever did. Some days she does quite well without tobacco, and other days it's harder for her to resist the nicotine cravings. But all in all, Mother's doing well."

"I'm happy to hear that you've stopped chewing," Eglin continued.

"There will be days when you'll crave nicotine fiercely. However, I know you can kick the tobacco habit. But if you slip and chew again, you'll stop again. It's never to late to stop, even if you have to stop a bunch of times. Eventually you'll make it."

"This is a wonderful day!" Eglin shouted. "Olive is now with the family again!"

Everyone except Plata came to greet Nicholas and Olive. Plata stayed away because her health had taken a turn for the worse. The cancer had grown, and the pain had become unbearable. It was necessary for Dr. Walkingstick to cut away some of her mouthparts. Sadly, he wasn't convinced that the cancer would stay away. Plata was very ill and disfigured now. She wasn't comfortable when anyone looked at her face, so Eglin and the others only caught faint glimpses of her as she hid in the shadows. Poor Plata! She may never realize her dreams of a mate or having little ladybugs. She might decide to stay in the shadows until the end.

Littleton was coming along nicely. His stomach ulcers were healing. Although he still had a strong desire for nicotine, Littleton was fighting the urge to return to the tobacco field and eat tobacco-poisoned aphids. He now loved the taste of sweet, healthy aphids. He often said, "The best aphids are pink and green — VERY TASTY! VERY TASTY, INDEED!" Sometimes, however, Littleton had stomach pains after eating the healthy aphids. Their sweet honeydew was too rich for his scarred stomach. But every day his health improved.

Happiness filled the little garden. Littleton, Ginny, Olive, and Plata were working to overcome their addiction to tobacco. Eglin and Varina were proud of them for trying.

Watching over his family and friends, Eglin felt both happy and sad. He was happy his family was together again. He was happy Varina's siblings were in the garden, too. However, Eglin felt sad because tobacco had taken Cousin Florence.

He missed Cousin Florence. And the saddest part was that it didn't have to happen. Her illness, as with all the tobacco-related sicknesses, was **preventable**. Florence didn't have to chew tobacco. Plata didn't have to dip snuff. And Madam Mouse and the mice didn't have to smoke. They didn't have to become sick and suffer.

Eglin looked to the sky. He was proud he had chosen never to use tobacco. He was healthy. He could walk, jump, play, and fly without any health problems interfering with what he wanted to do. He could take deep breaths of fresh air and enjoy the wonderful feeling of blowing it back out again. He didn't cough frequently, he didn't have sores in his mouth or air passages, and he didn't have chest pains. He was healthy. Eglin was enjoying life.

Turning his attention to the future, Eglin smiled. He knew there was another reason why he was happy. Nicholas and Olive had brought a friend to the garden. She was a beautiful long-horned grasshopper with the most attractive coloring and long, flowing antennae. She would make a good mate.

Without taking his eyes off the female grasshopper, Eglin straightened his antennae. He proudly puffed out his chest and stood tall. Then, as nature intended, Eglin rubbed the upper parts of his front wings together, filling the garden with a romantic mating song. He smiled. Surely the female long-horn would hear his call and walk his way. After all, Eglin was the eldest brother, the best jumper, healthy and tobacco-free, and, as long-horned grasshoppers go, the best catch in all of Nightshade County.

Glossary

ad·dic·tive drug (ə DIK´ tiv drug) n. A drug (narcotic) which is habit-forming, making the user want more. Users often are unable to stop even when they want to.

an·ten·nae (an TEN´ē) n. 1. The plural of **antenna**. 2. The movable feelers located on the heads of certain arthropods.

aphid (Ā´ fid) n. Any of a large family of small, soft-bodied insects that suck the juices from plants; a plant louse. Of the Aphididae family.

asth·ma (AZ´m ə) n. a health condition caused by an allergy or the inhalation of dangerous substances, accompanied by coughing, difficulty in breathing, and a suffocating feeling.

ben·zene (BEN´ zēn) n. A clear, flammable, poisonous liquid, used to make plastics, insecticides, detergents, paints, etc.

brain attack (brān ə TAK´) n. Another description for a stroke. Any sudden attack of disease or illness, especially paralysis or cerebral (brain) accident.

bron·chi·tis (bran KIT´ is) n. An infection, reddening, heat, pain, and swelling of the mucous lining of the bronchial tubes (the tubes that connect the windpipe to the lungs).

can·cer (KAN´ s ə r) n. 1. (a) A malignant growth in the body of a person or animal; tumors tend to spread locally to other parts of the body. (b) Any of various diseases with uncontrolled growth of cells that disrupt body tissue.

car·bon mon·ox·ide n. A colorless, odorless, highly poisonous gas, produced by the incomplete burning of materials containing carbon; it burns with a pale-blue flame.

chew (choo) n. 1. Shredded tobacco for chewing. v. To bite and grind or crush with the teeth.

cur·ing shed (KYOOR ing shed) n. The place where tobacco is processed by drying and/or aging.

dip·ping (DIP ing) v. 1. To put snuff (ground tobacco) on the gums. 2. To put into or under liquid. 3. To clean or bathe (sheep, dogs, hogs) in disinfectant.

elephant-hide disease n. (Slang) The term used in this book to refer to the disease called leukoplakia, a gum-and-tongue disease caused by chewing tobacco or dipping snuff and holding the juices in the mouth. A pre-cancerous growth that looks like a wrinkled, white, leathery patch, resembling an elephant's hide.

em·phy·sema (em f ə SĒ´m ə) n. A severe lung disease where the walls of the air sacs lose flexibility and are destroyed. Stale air becomes trapped, and the lungs swell. Blood flow is disrupted, and the heart beats faster, sometimes causing the heart to become enlarged.

ex·o·skel·e·ton (eks ō SKEL´ ə t ə n) n. Any hard, external, supporting structure, as the shells of oysters and lobsters or the shells of insects or spiders.

form·al·de·hyde (for MAL´d ə hid´) A sharp and pungent gas used in solutions as a strong disinfectant and preservative, and in the making of synthetic resins, dyes, etc.

in·sec·ti·cide (in SEK´t ə sīd) n. Any substance used to kill insects.

leu·ko·pla·ki·a (loo kō PLA´ ke ə) n. A disease, sometimes precancerous, that produces thick, leathery, wrinkled, white patches covering the gums, tongue, and cheeks.

molt (mōlt) v. To shed off the exoskeleton, hair, outer skin, horns, or feathers at certain intervals, before new growth.

nic·o·tine (NIK´ ə tēn) n. A poisonous substance found in tobacco leaves which causes the habit-forming quality of tobacco; (also used in insecticides).

night·shade (NIT shad) n. 1. Any of a chiefly tropical plant family with five-lobed leaves and flowers of various colors 2. A large family of poisonous and nonpoisonous plants, chiefly in warm regions, having round stems, rank smell, and watery sap. Includes tobacco, red peppers, tomatoes, potatoes, petunias, and eggplants.

nymph (nimf) n. The young of an insect before metamorphosis; may look totally different from the adult or may look similar to the adult parent.

palp or **pal·pus** (palp) (PAL´ pes) n. A jointed organ or feeler for touching or tasting, attached to one of the head appendages of insects, lobsters, etc.

pneu·mo·nia (noo MŌN´y ə) n. An inflammation or infection of the lungs caused by bacteria, viruses, etc.

pre·vent·able (prē VENT´ ə bul) adj. Something that didn't have to happen.

secondhand smoke n. The smoke which comes from tobacco that other people are smoking, including (a) the smoke which is blown out after a person puffs on a cigarette, cigar, or pipe, (b) the smoke that comes from a burning cigarette, cigar, or pipe. Both contain the same poisonous chemicals as the smoke inhaled when a person smokes.

snuff n. 1. A preparation of powdered or ground tobacco that is inhaled by sniffing, chewing, or rubbing on the gums. 2. Any powder taken by inhaling. 3. The act or sound of snuffing: sniff v. 1. To draw in through the nose; inhale strongly; sniff. 2. To put out with snuffers or by pinching (as in putting out a candle).

spi·ra·cles (SPI r ə k ə lz) n 1. Small breathing holes (airholes) of arthropods, usually located along the thorax and abdomen and usually in pairs totaling ten airholes. 2. The airholes of whales, dolphins, porpoises, and other large marine mammals.

stroke (strōk) n. Any sudden attack of disease or illness, especially paralysis or brain accident.

to·bacco tar (t ə BAK′ ō tar) n.
The solid which comes from tobacco
smoke. A brown sticky substance in
tobacco leaves.

tu·mor (T͞OO′ m ə r) n. (a) A swelling
on some part of the body. (b) A
mass of new growth not part of the
surrounding organ or tissue, having
no function: such tumors are either
benign (noncancerous) or malignant
(cancerous).

wad   n. A lump or small compact
mass of something, such as chewing
tobacco.

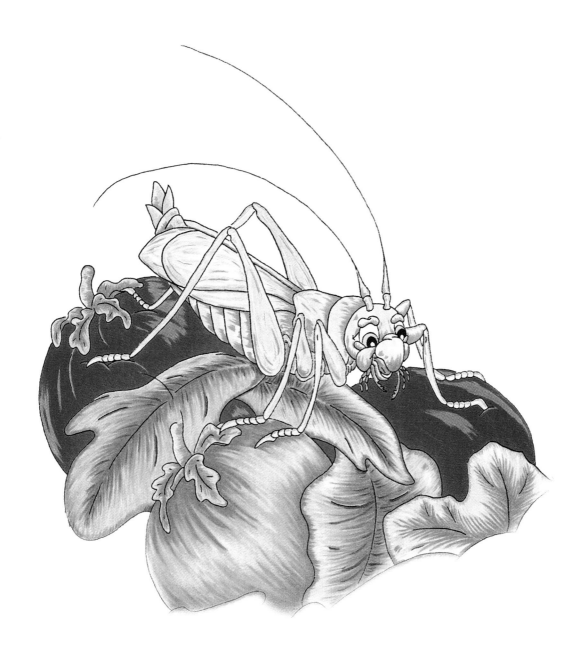

Be Like Eglin and Choose to be Tobacco-Free!

About The Author

Debra L.Wert was born in Washington, D.C., and now makes her home in Central Florida. She is a graduate of the University of Maryland, where she earned a Bachelor of Arts degree in Art Education. After many years in the education and business fields, she decided to pursue a lifelong dream to write children's books.

When Debra was 22 years old, she watched her grandmother, who always had a cigarette in her mouth, die of lung cancer. When her grandmother was in the hospital, Debra sat with her. The night before she died, the sick woman relived her life as she told her granddaughter stories about the good old days. Debra has always remembered her grandmother's last words about cigarettes. She said over and over again, "Those horrible things. If you're smart, you'll never start smoking them." Debra has taken her grandmother's advice.

Mac's Choice, Debra's first published work, has been a tremendous success. It teaches young children the harmful effects of experimenting with and using illegal drugs. Debra is hoping that ***Eglin Long-Horn of Nightshade County*** will be as helpful in giving children the knowledge they need to make informed, responsible choices regarding their health and personal decisions concerning whether to use tobacco products or not use them. She hopes her readers will make the wise and healthy choice and choose to be tobacco-free.

Books by Debra L. Wert

Mac's Choice (substance-abuse prevention)
Mac's Choice Workbook
Caterfly, Mac's Back (substance-abuse prevention)
Caterfly, Mac's Back A Teacher's Guide
Eglin Long-Horn of Nightshade County (tobacco-use prevention)
Eglin Long-Horn of Nightshade County A Teacher's Guide

OTHER HELP FOR CHILDREN BOOKS
by
ROCKY RIVER PUBLISHERS

MAC'S CHOICE
MAC'S CHOICE Workbook
Nationally acclaimed books for educating young children on the dangers of using drugs. Received a four-star rating for drug education. Ages 6 - 12.

CATERFLY, MAC'S BACK Struggling to Stay Drug-Free
CATERFLY, MAC'S BACK A Teacher's Guide
A substance-abuse prevention storybook and teacher's guide. Ages 10 - 12. To educate children about the hazards of drug use before they arrive at middle school. These materials are receiving outstanding reviews from educators.

HELP FOR CHILDREN, From Infancy to Adulthood, 6th Ed.
An indispensable national reference for all those whose work involves children.

STRESS STOPPERS for CHILDREN and ADOLESCENTS, 2nd Ed.
A book to help children and adolescents learn how to deal with stress.

ALEXANDRA, KEEPER of DREAMS
A story about the importance of holding onto your dreams. Ages 6 - 10. Alexandra is a very determined little duck with a big dream. Beautifully illustrated for the young reader. *Alexandra, Keeper of Dreams* was awarded first place by the PIVA of Virginia.

HENRIETTA
Henrietta is an ostrich that is afraid of practically everything. Ages 6 - 10. A delight to read, filled with beautiful graphics, and *Henrietta* teaches an important lesson about dealing with fears. Henrietta's art was part of the Distinguished Original Art displayed at the Bardean Gallery in New Mexico and is listed in New Mexico's Collector's Guide.

If you wish to place an order, obtain further information, or request a free catalog, please write or call:

Rocky River Publishers
P.O. Box 1679
Shepherdstown, WV 25443

(304) 876-2711
(800) 343-0686